Home Safari

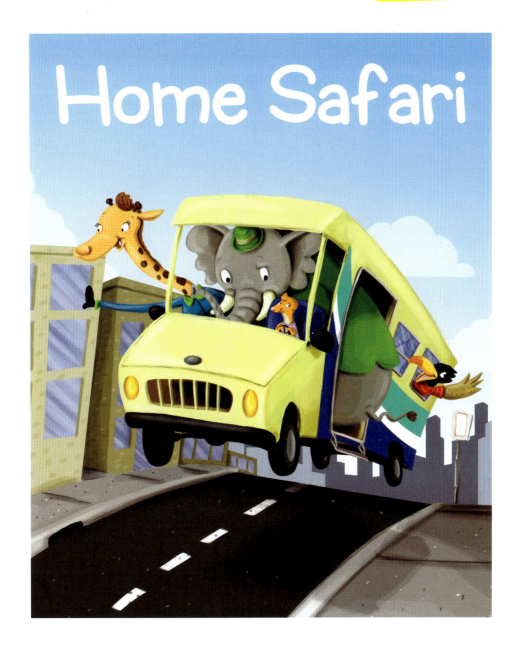

By Mary Kate Bolinder
Illustrated by Brian Martin

Publishing Credits

Rachelle Cracchiolo, M.S.Ed., *Publisher*
Aubrie Nielsen, M.S.Ed., *EVP of Content Development*
Emily R. Smith, M.A.Ed., *VP of Content Development*
Véronique Bos, *Creative Director*
Dani Neiley, *Associate Editor*
Kevin Pham, *Graphic Designer*

Image Credits

Illustrated by Brian Martin

Library of Congress Cataloging-in-Publication Data

Names: Bolinder, Mary Kate, author. | Martin, Brian (Brian Michael), 1978- illustrator.
Title: Home safari / by Mary Kate Bolinder ; illustrated by Brian Martin.
Description: Huntington Beach, CA : Teacher Created Materials, [2022] | Audience: Grades 2-3. | Summary: ""Four savanna animals set off on an adventure to see how people live around the world. What kinds of homes will these friends find?""-- Provided by publisher.
Identifiers: LCCN 2021052868 (print) | LCCN 2021052869 (ebook) | ISBN 9781087601892 (paperback) | ISBN 9781087631943 (ebook)
Subjects: LCSH: Readers (Primary) | LCGFT: Readers (Publications)
Classification: LCC PE1119.2 .B654 2022 (print) | LCC PE1119.2 (ebook) | DDC 428.6/2--dc23/eng/20211109
LC record available at https://lccn.loc.gov/2021052868
LC ebook record available at https://lccn.loc.gov/2021052869"

5482 Argosy Avenue
Huntington Beach, CA 92649
www.tcmpub.com

ISBN 978-1-0876-0189-2

Printed by 51250
PO 10851 / Printed in USA

Table of Contents

Chapter One

Here We Go!

Giraffe, Elephant, and Meerkat walked through the savanna.

"I'm bored," said Giraffe.

"Me too," huffed Elephant. "All I see are trees and grass every day."

"I'm bored too," said Hornbill as he landed on a nearby tree. "I've flown all over the savanna, but I want to see more of the world!"

Just then, a large car pulled up. People hopped out to take pictures of the animals.

"I want to go on a safari too," Hornbill said.

Like magic, a second car appeared next to the tree. Hornbill squawked and almost fell off his branch.

"Look!" said Meerkat. "Hop in, and we can go on our own safari!"

The animals climbed into the big car.

"Hold on tight!" said Meerkat.

"How exciting! Where should we go?" asked Giraffe.

"Let's go see where the humans live," said Meerkat. "Maybe we will find a new place to live, too!"

"What kind of car is this?" asked Hornbill.

"This is called a motor home," said Meerkat. "It is a house on wheels with a bathroom, a kitchen, and a bed. Everything we need!"

"A house on wheels?" said Elephant. "I don't think I like this!"

"Don't be silly," said Hornbill. "We can take this magical house wherever we want to go. It will be a fun adventure."

"Yes," said Giraffe. "I want to see lots of different houses. Where will we go first?"

"First stop is a city!" said Meerkat. "Here we go!"

The motor home began to shake…

Chapter Two

Homes on Land

Suddenly, the four animals were in a new place. They looked out the windows.

"Look at that! What are those tall things? They go higher in the sky than you do, Hornbill," said Elephant.

"That is a skyscraper," said Meerkat. "It is a tall building with a lot of rooms inside it. A skyscraper can have many apartments. An apartment is a home inside a large building. It can have one room or many rooms."

"I've never been to the city before," said Giraffe.

"We've never been anywhere but the savanna," said Hornbill.

"The city is a crowded place. There are many large buildings close together. And many people live there," said Meerkat.

"Where are we going next?" asked Giraffe.

"Next stop is the suburbs," said Meerkat. "That is an area outside a city. It is not as crowded as the city. Sometimes, there is a yard to play in."

The motor home shook again, and the animals found themselves in a new location. They were now on a small street lined with houses. The animals looked out the windows of the motor home.

"These houses come in all shapes and sizes," said Elephant. "But I do not see a home that is big enough for me."

"Oh, look in that tree next to the house! What is that?" asked Giraffe.

"That is a tree house," said Meerkat. "Not many people around the world live in a tree house, but it can be a fun place to play."

"I want to live there!" said Hornbill. "Then, I could live in a large home in the trees."

"I could visit you there," said Giraffe. "I am tall enough to reach the top of a tree."

"It still looks too small for me," said Elephant.

The friends started driving along until they came to a large house with a tall gate.

"What is this place?" asked Giraffe. "It looks so big!"

"This is a mansion," said Meerkat. "A mansion is a very big house with many rooms. I've heard that some mansions can have movie theaters, bowling alleys, or even indoor swimming pools!"

"Wow!" said Hornbill. "Elephant, do you think a mansion would be big enough for you?"

"No," sighed Elephant. "The biggest house I've ever seen is still not big enough for me."

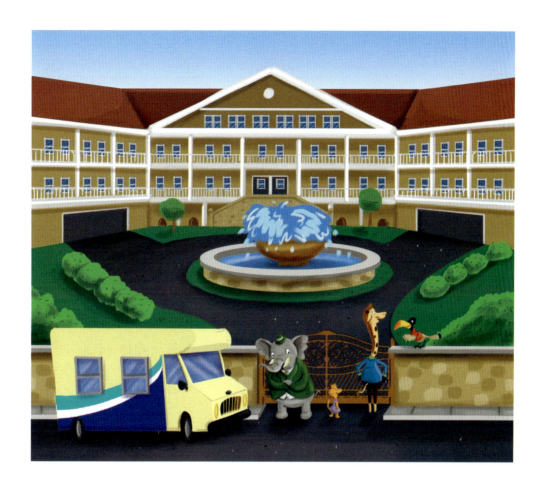

"Don't worry," said Meerkat. "There are still more homes to see. We will find a home you will like. Next, let's see some homes near water."

The motor home shook again, and Elephant almost fell over.

Chapter Three

Homes by the Water

Now, they were next to a river. All the animal friends climbed out to look at what was floating on the water.

"Meerkat, what is that thing?" asked Giraffe.

"That is the next stop on our safari!" said Meerkat. "It is a houseboat. It is a lot like the motor home, except it floats on water. It has all the room we need and can take us wherever we want to go. Climb aboard!"

"I think I am too heavy for this boat! What if it sinks?" asked Elephant.

"Be brave, Elephant!" said Hornbill. "Trying new things is part of this adventure."

The animal friends headed down the river until they came to a small group of houses near the shore.

"Look at those houses!" said Hornbill. "It looks like they have legs!"